CAMILA
THE SPELLING BEE STAR

written by ALICIA SALAZAR

illustrated by MÁRIO GUSHIKEN

cover artwork by THAIS DAMIÃO

PICTURE WINDOW BOOKS
a capstone imprint

Published by Picture Window Books, an imprint of Capstone
1710 Roe Crest Drive, North Mankato, Minnesota 56003
capstonepub.com

Library of Congress Cataloging-in-Publication Data
Names: Salazar, Alicia, 1973- author. | Gushiken, Mário, illustrator. |
Damião, Thais, artist.
Title: Camila the spelling bee star / written by Alicia Salazar ; illustrated by Mário Gushiken ; cover artwork by Thais Damião.
Description: North Mankato, Minnesota : Picture Window Books, [2023] |
Series: Camila the star | Audience: Ages 5-7. | Audience: Grades K-1. |
Summary: At first Camila is thrilled to be chosen to represent her class in the school spelling bee, but than she becomes anxious about performing in front of an audience and considers withdrawing.
Identifiers: LCCN 2022029015 (print) | LCCN 2022029016 (ebook) |
ISBN 9781484670958 (hardcover) | ISBN 9781484670910 (paperback) |
ISBN 9781484670927 (pdf) | ISBN 9781484670989 (kindle edition)
Subjects: LCSH: Hispanic American girls—Juvenile fiction. | Spelling bees—Juvenile fiction. | Performance anxiety—Juvenile fiction. | Courage—Juvenile fiction. | CYAC: Hispanic Americans—Fiction. | Spelling bees—Fiction. | Stage fright—Fiction. | Courage—Fiction. | LCGFT: Picture books.
Classification: LCC PZ7.1.S2483 Cax 2023 (print) | LCC PZ7.1.S2483 (ebook) |
DDC [E]—dc23
LC record available at https://lccn.loc.gov/2022029015
LC ebook record available at https://lccn.loc.gov/2022029016

Designer: Hilary Wacholz

TABLE OF CONTENTS

Meet Camila and Her Family

Papá

Mamá

Ana, age 14

Andres, age 10

Camila, age 7

Spanish Glossary

almohada (ahl-moh-AH-dah)—pillow

brazos (BRAH-sohs)—arms

concurso de ortografía (kohn-KOOR-soh DEH ohr-toh-grah-FEE-ah)—spelling bee

estómago (ehs-TOH-mah-goh)—stomach

Mamá (mah-MAH)—Mom

mente (MEHN-the)—mind

no puedo (NOH PWAY-doh)—I can't

nubes (NOO-behs)—clouds

si puedo (SEE PWAY-doh)—I can

Chapter 1

THE BEST SPELLER

"Camila," said Mrs. Jolly, "as the best speller in the class, you will represent us in the school spelling bee."

Camila jumped up and down.

"Yes! I love spelling!" she said. "If I win, will I be a star?"

"You are already a star for having the courage to try," said Mrs. Jolly.

Camila beamed.

"I'm going to be in the **concurso de ortografía**," she told her family when she got home.

Her friends and family promised to come watch her compete.

Camila was happy . . . until she went to bed.

With her head on her **almohada**, she started seeing pictures in her mind. There were hundreds of people, watching her.

What if she spelled a word wrong?

What if her mind went blank?

What if she forgot how to talk?

The next day Camila told Mrs. Jolly that she didn't want to compete.

"Are you nervous?" asked Mrs. Jolly.

"I'm afraid my **mente** will go blank in front of everyone I know," said Camila.

"I want you to think about it over the weekend," Mrs. Jolly said. "Remember, you are a star no matter what."

Chapter 2
CAMILA'S ANXIETY

Over the weekend, Camila worked on memorizing her word list. She highlighted the suffixes and prefixes. She grouped the nouns together.

Then the verbs.

Then the describing words.

Her sister helped her practice. "Circus," Ana called out.

Camila imagined standing in front of a big crowd of everyone she knew.

"Circus," she said. "C . . ."

She imagined everybody
shaking their heads.

"I . . . ," Camila said.

She imagined everybody
laughing.

"**No puedo**," said Camila.
"I have to quit."

"Do you feel like you can't breathe and you want to run away and hide?" asked Ana.

Camila nodded, hunching her shoulders.

"You have anxiety," said Ana. "Take deep breaths and imagine yourself winning."

Camila closed her eyes and imagined herself on stage.

"**Si puedo**," she whispered to herself.

Then, the pictures in her mind changed. Everyone in the crowd was pointing and laughing.

Her **estómago** felt sick.

Camila thought about what Mrs. Jolly said. She was already a star. And stars have the courage to try.

Chapter 3

CALM AND CONFIDENT

On Sunday morning, Camila searched "help for anxiety" on the computer.

She found a word she had never seen before.

Mindfulness.

Mindfulness meant that you let your scary thoughts float by like **nubes**.

You didn't let them stop you.

Camila's heart beat faster.

"Maybe I can do this," she thought.

She closed her eyes. Everyone was laughing. She watched the picture float by.

She was so scared, she wanted to crawl in bed and forget about the spelling bee.

But she watched the picture
until it went away.

She tried again and again.

On Monday morning, she told Mrs. Jolly she would be in the spelling bee. She was still scared, but she had to try.

The day of the spelling bee, Camila stood on the stage. She looked out into the crowd.

The scary pictures came back to her **mente**. She imagined everyone pointing and laughing.

She wanted to run off the stage and into **Mamá's brazos**.

But she watched the pictures until they went away.

She did it over and over.

Mrs. Jolly called out the last word.

"Courage," said Camila. "C-O-U-R-A-G-E. Courage."

"That is correct," said Ms. Jolly.

The principal walked to the stage and shook her hand.

The crowd clapped.

"Congratulations, Camila,"
said Principal Weber. "I admire
how calm and confident you
behaved."

Camila took a deep breath
and let it out slowly.

"I was really scared," said Camila. "But I didn't let that stop me from being a star for my courage *and* for my spelling."

Breathing with a Buddy

When Camila was nervous about the spelling bee, she used mindfulness to calm herself. She imagined the things that made her nervous as clouds floating away. You can try doing the same thing to calm yourself down when you are worried about something. Or try this breathing activity. It will leave you feeling calmer and energized.

WHAT YOU NEED

- a stuffed animal
- room to lay down comfortably

WHAT YOU DO

1. Lay down on your back on a firm surface like the floor or a bed.

2. Set your stuffed animal on your belly.

3. Breathe normally. Your stuffed buddy will only move a little bit.

4. Now breathe deeply enough so that both your lungs and tummy expand. With a deep breath, your buddy should move upward. Hold your breath for a moment, then slowly blow it out.

5. Repeat this four more times.

Does focusing on your deep breaths help you feel calmer? You can also imagine that you are blowing your worries away, one by one, when you let out your breaths.

Glossary

anxiety (ang-ZYE-uh-tee)—a feeling of worry or fear

compete (kuhm-PEET)—to try hard to outdo others at a race or contest

courage (KUHR-ij)—bravery during hard times

confident (KON-fuh-duhnt)—sure of oneself

memorize (MEM-uh-ryze)—to learn by heart

mindfulness (MYND-fuhl-nis)—paying full attention to something, often by slowing down to notice what you are doing and how you are feeling

prefix (PREE-fiks)—a group of letters at the beginning of a word that has a meaning of its own

represent (rep-ri-ZENT)—to serve as an example of a group

suffix (SUHF-iks)—a group of letters at the end of a word that has a meaning of its own

Think About the Story

1. Camila prepared to be in the spelling bee. What are some of the things she did to get ready for the big day?

2. Talk about feeling nervous. What is something that makes you nervous? How did your body feel when you were nervous? How do you deal with your nervous feelings?

3. In the story, Camila imagined the pictures in her mind as clouds that floated away. Draw a cloud picture of one or two things that you worry about, then imagine them floating away.

4. Imagine you are a reporter, and write a story about the results of the school spelling bee.

About the Author

Alicia Salazar is a Mexican American children's book author who has written for blogs, magazines, and educational publishers. She was also once an elementary school teacher and a marine biologist. She currently lives in the suburbs of Houston, Texas, but is a city girl at heart. When Alicia is not dreaming up new adventures to experience, she is turning her adventures into stories for kids.

About the Illustrator

Mário Gushiken has been working as an illustrator since 2014. While he currently works mainly on book publishing projects, he has worked in the editorial, animation, advertising, and fashion industries. In his spare time, Mario likes to hang out with friends and play video games.